EUOPLOCEPHALUS

CARNOTAURUS

TROPEOGNATHUS

PARASAUROLOPHUS

BRACHIOSAURUS

DILOPHOSAURUS

GALLIMIMUS

STYRACOSAURUS

VELOCIRAPTOR

TUOJIANGOSAURUS

JANE YOLEN

# How Do Dinosaurs

## Get Well Soon?

*Illustrated by*

MARK TEAGUE

THE BLUE SKY PRESS

An Imprint of Scholastic Inc. · New York

THE BLUE SKY PRESS

Text copyright © 2003 by Jane Yolen

Illustrations copyright © 2003 by Mark Teague

All rights reserved.

Library of Congress card catalog number: 2002006575

ISBN-13: 978-0-545-02739-7

ISBN-10: 0-545-02739-X

12 11 10 9 8 7 6 5 4 3 2 1     07 08 09 10 11

Printed in Singapore                    46

This edition first printing, June 2007

Designed by Kathleen Westray

To David Francis Stemple, my first grandson

J. Y.

To Bonnie and Robbie, for dreaming of dinosaurs

M. T.

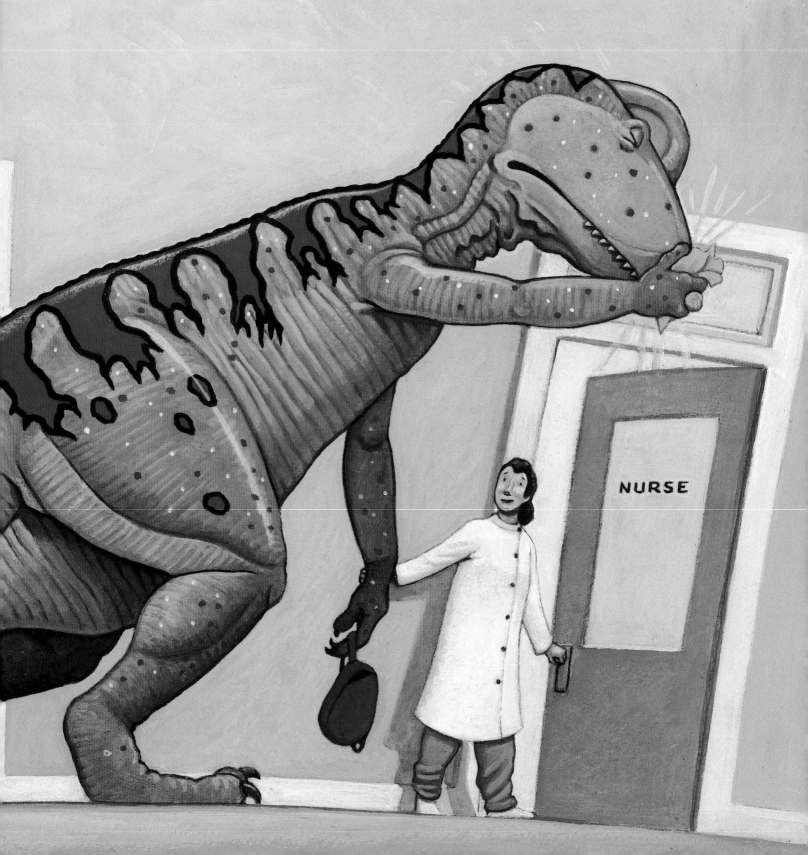

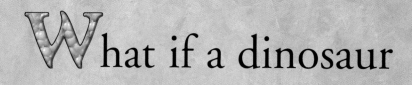

What if a dinosaur

catches the flu?

Does he whimper and whine

in between each *Atchoo*?

NURSE

Does he drop

dirty tissues

all over

the floor?

GALLIMIMUS

Does he fling

all his medicine

out of the door?

Does he flip off
his covers
with tooth
and with tail?

EUOPLOCEPHALUS

Does he

dump out

his juice

and get sick

in a pail?

BRACHIOSAURUS

DOES A

DINOSAUR

WAIL?

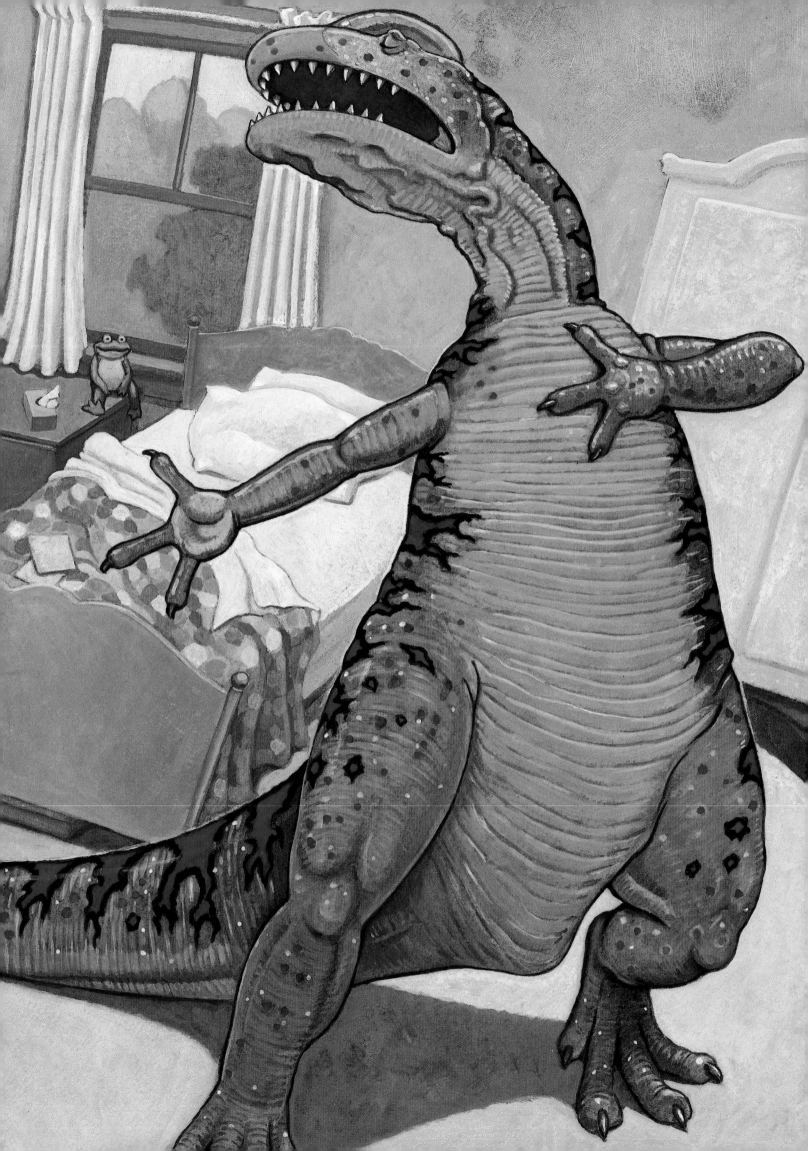

What if a dinosaur
goes to the doc?

Does he drag all his feet
till his mom is in shock?

CARNOTAURUS

Does he hold his mouth closed when he's told, "Open wide"?

Does he scream?

Is he mean?

Does he run off

and hide?

Does he
push back each drink,
spit his pills in the sink?

Does he
make a big stink?
Is that what you think?

No . . .

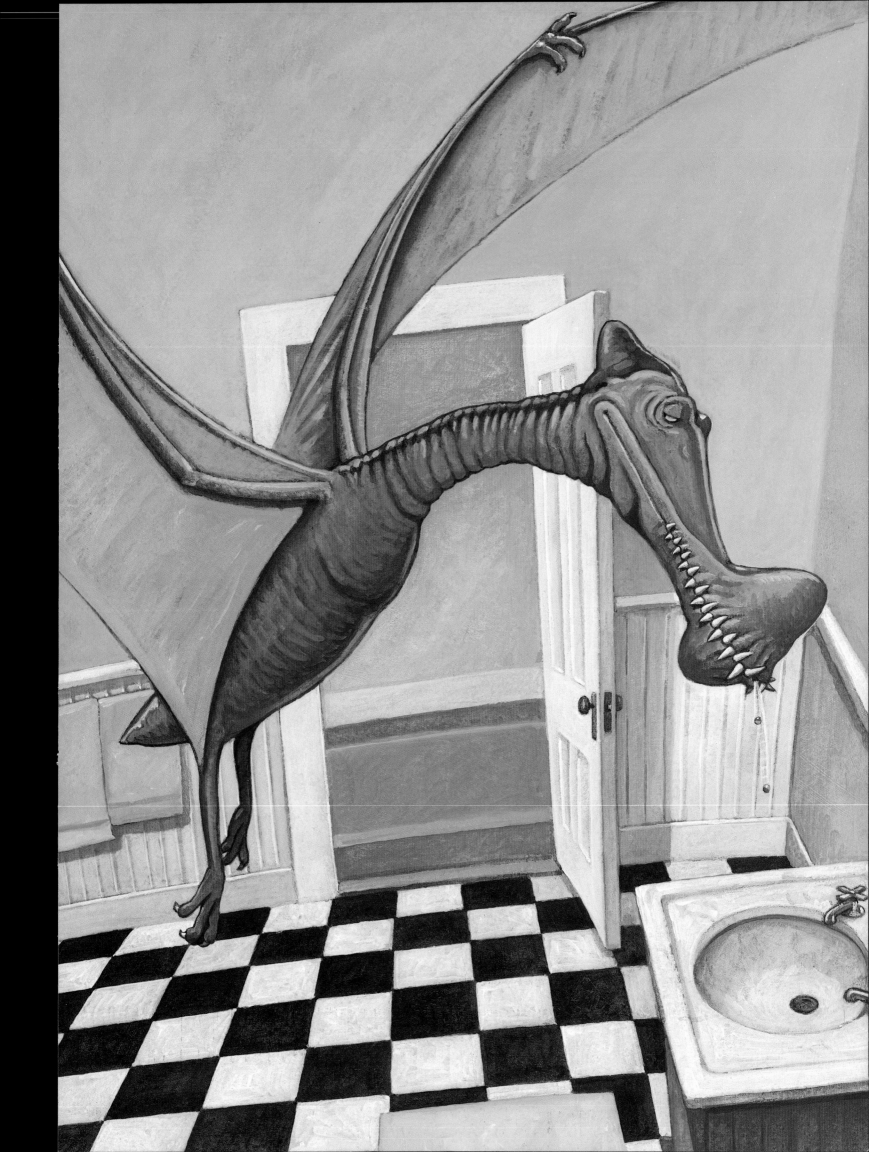

He drinks lots of juice,
and he gets lots of rest.

He's good at the doctor's,
'cause doctors know best.

He uses a hankie
on mouth
and on nose.
He snuggles
right down
underneath
the bedclothes.

He takes all his medicine

without a fight.

DIPLODOCUS

He closes his eyes.
He whispers good night.

Then Mama and Papa
tiptoe out the door.

Get well.

Get well, little dinosaur.

EUOPLOCEPHALUS

CARNOTAURUS

TROPEOGNATHUS

PARASAUROLOPHUS

BRACHIOSAURUS

DILOPHOSAURUS

GALLIMIMUS

STYRACOSAURUS

VELOCIRAPTOR

TUOJIANGOSAURUS